THE WITCH AT NO. 13

Kites

TAKE OFF WITH A KITE!

This lively series is designed for children who have developed reading fluency and enjoy reading complete books on their own.

The stories are attractively presented with plenty of illustrations which make them satisfying and fun! A perfect follow-on from the Read Alone series.

GU00802408

Other Kites by the same author (in reading order)

THE GHOST AT NO. 13
THE HICCUPS AT NO. 13
THE MERMAID AT NO. 13
THE HULLABALOO AT NO. 13

Some other Kites for you to enjoy

BONESHAKER   Paul and Emma Rogers
DUMBELLINA   Brough Girling
THE INTERGALACTIC KITCHEN
  Frank Rodgers
JASON BROWN – FROG   Len Gurd
KING KEITH AND THE JOLLY LODGER
  Kaye Umansky
MR MAJEIKA   Humphrey Carpenter
NUTS   Noel Ford
OVER THE MOON AND FAR AWAY
  Margaret Nash
SEPTIMOUSE, SUPERMOUSE!
  Ann Jungman
TOMMY NINER AND THE PLANET OF
  DANGER   Tony Bradman

GYLES BRANDRETH

THE WITCH
AT NO. 13

ILLUSTRATED BY SALLY ROBSON

VIKING

For Aphra,
who read it first

VIKING

Published by the Penguin Group
Penguin Books Ltd, 27 Wrights Lane, London W8 5TZ, England
Penguin Books USA Inc., 375 Hudson Street, New York, New York 10014, USA
Penguin Books Australia Ltd, Ringwood, Victoria, Australia
Penguin Books Canada Ltd, 10 Alcorn Avenue, Toronto, Ontario, Canada
    M4V 3B2
Penguin Books (NZ) Ltd, 182–190 Wairau Road, Auckland 10, New Zealand

Penguin Books Ltd, Registered Offices: Harmondsworth, Middlesex, England

First published 1995
10 9 8 7 6 5 4 3 2 1

Text copyright © Gyles Brandreth, 1995
Illustrations copyright © Sally Robson, 1995

Filmset in Linotron Palatino 14/22 pt by
Rowland Phototypesetting Ltd, Bury St Edmunds, Suffolk
Made and printed in Great Britain by Butler & Tanner Ltd, Frome and London

A CIP catalogue record for this book is available from the British Library

ISBN 0–670–85443–3

1. Spilt Milk

Hamlet Orlando Julius Caesar Brown had a problem. And it wasn't his name. It was Puddles.

Hamlet lived at No. 13 Irving Terrace, Hammersmith, West London, with his mother, his father, his goody-goody eleven-year-old sister Susan, and a large, friendly, fluffy, snuffly puppy called Puddles.

Puddles was called Puddles for a very obvious reason. He kept making them.

Hamlet was called Hamlet Orlando Julius Caesar Brown because Mr and Mrs Brown were both actors, and in the year Hamlet was born Mr Brown had played the parts of Hamlet, Orlando and Julius Caesar in three famous plays by William Shakespeare.

In the year Susan was born Mr and Mrs Brown had appeared together in a pantomime of *Aladdin*. Mr Brown had played the part of Aladdin's wicked Uncle Abanazar. Mrs Brown had played the part of the beautiful Princess Badroulboudour.

"Let's call our baby Badroulboudour," said Mr Brown. "It's a lovely name."

"It's a silly name," said Mrs Brown. "We'll call her Susan." And they did.

10

Susan was perfect. She was pretty. She was kind. She was clever. At school, she was always top of the class. At home, she was always working on a project. She had just finished a project on African animals. Mrs Lilley said it was the best project she had seen in fourteen years as a teacher. Mr and Mrs Brown were very proud of their daughter.

"This is a beautifully presented piece of work," said Mr Brown, admiring Susan's drawing of a rhinoceros. "I never knew the horn of a rhinoceros was made of hair, not bone."

"I like the picture of the zebra best," said Mrs Brown.

"A zebra's stripes are as different as a human being's fingerprints," said Susan. "No two zebras have the same stripes."

"Well, I *never*!" said Mrs Brown.

"I have a wonderful daughter!"

exclaimed Mr Brown. "She is both fair and wise."

Mr Brown talked as if he was standing on a stage acting in an extraordinary play even when he was standing in the kitchen at No. 13 Irving Terrace making a very ordinary Saturday morning breakfast.

"What's your favourite animal?" asked Mrs Brown.

"The duck-billed platypus," said Susan. "It can eat its own weight in worms every day."

"Ugh!" said Mr Brown, scooping some hot baked beans on to a slice of toast.

"Boring!" said Hamlet rather rudely.

Susan decided to ignore her brother. "My second favourite is the hippopotamus. A hippopotamus can run faster than a human being."

"Boring!" said Hamlet again, more loudly this time.

"And my third favourite," Susan
continued, "is the giraffe. Did you know
that a giraffe is more than a metre taller
than a double-decker bus?"

"That's interesting," said Mrs Brown.

"That's boring," said Hamlet.

"Come along now, Hamlet," said Mr
Brown, "there's no need to be rude."

"I hate know-alls," said Hamlet.

"And I hate know-nothings," said
Susan.

"And what I really hate are know-alls

13

who show off all the time," said Hamlet.

Mrs Brown was about to say firmly, "Now stop it, you two," when the kitchen door was pushed open and there stood Puddles with his tail wagging. He gave a little bark as if to say, "Here I am and aren't I a clever boy?"

"Oh dear," said Mr Brown, "I think he's done it again."

"If he has," said Mrs Brown, "he'll have to go. Enough's enough."

"I'll go and see," said Hamlet, and he got up from the kitchen table and walked out into the hallway. Sure enough, there, right in the middle of the hallway floor, was a great big puddle.

"Naughty Puddles," said Hamlet, coming back into the kitchen and going to fetch the mop.

"Naughty, naughty Puddles," said Mr Brown, wagging his finger at the little dog, who wagged his tail back and barked happily.

"I'm sorry," said Mrs Brown, "I know he's only a puppy and he's very sweet, but we can't have him making puddles all over the house all day long. Unless you can get him to behave himself, he's going to have to go."

"No, Mum, please," said Hamlet.

"Mum's right," said Susan.

"Mind your own business," said Hamlet.

"It *is* my business," said Susan. "He made a puddle in *my* room on Tuesday."

"And who cleared it up?" asked Hamlet.

"You did," said Susan, "and quite right too. He's your dog."

"He's only a puppy," said Mr Brown. "He'll grow out of it."

"Only if he's properly trained," said Mrs Brown.

"Exactly," said Mr Brown. "And, as you know, I have taken personal charge of this young beagle's training and he's coming along nicely. Watch!"

Mr Brown held up a little bit of bacon and said, "Sit, Puddles, sit."

Puddles didn't sit. Puddles began leaping up and down, his tail wagging more excitedly than ever.

Mr Brown waved the bit of bacon in
front of the puppy and said, "Now beg,
Puddles, beg."

Puddles didn't beg. Instead Puddles
jumped up on to Hamlet's chair and then
jumped straight on to the kitchen table,
plonking his paws on Mr Brown's
breakfast plate and at the same time
knocking over the carton of milk.

17

"Oh dear," said Mr Brown. "He doesn't seem to have got the knack of it yet."

"I am very, very cross," said Mrs Brown. And she sounded very cross. Even Puddles could tell she wasn't pleased. His tail stopped wagging.

"It's not his fault, Mum," said Hamlet, who was trying to mop up the spilt milk with a damp cloth.

"The boy is right," said Mr Brown, picking up Puddles and tucking the puppy under his arm.

"If it isn't his fault, whose fault is it then?" asked Mrs Brown sternly.

"Mine!" said Hamlet.

"Mine!" said Mr Brown.

Susan said nothing.

Mrs Brown sighed and said, "I'll give him one more chance. If this time next week he's still leaving puddles all over

the house and jumping up on to tables
and knocking things over he'll have to
go. Is that clearly understood?"

"Yes, Mum," said Hamlet.

"Yes, dear," said Mr Brown.

"Good!" said Mrs Brown. "Now,
while I go upstairs to finish recording
the new book for Mrs Mayhew, I suggest
you go to the library and get out a simple
book on how to house-train a beagle
puppy."

"Yes, dear," said Mr Brown.

"And be sure to clear up this mess
before you go."

"Yes, dear," said Mr Brown.

Mrs Brown left her husband and
children to tidy up in the kitchen and
went upstairs to the spare room where
she kept her tape recorder. Mrs Mayhew
was the old lady who lived at No. 17
Irving Terrace. She was almost blind and

could not read any more, so every now and then Mrs Brown recorded a book for her.

"Your mother's right," said Mr Brown, who was still holding Puddles under his arm while he tried to clear away the breakfast things. "We've got to train this scallywag properly. We'll set off for the library right away."

"Can I come too?" asked Susan.

"What do you want from the library?" asked Hamlet, who would have been much happier if his goody-goody know-all sister had stayed at home.

"Some books for my new project."

"Excellent, dear daughter," said Mr Brown. "Is this another project about animals?"

"No," said Susan. "This one's different. This one is all about witches."

2. Droopy Drawers

As Mr Brown, Hamlet and Susan set off
for the library, Puddles led the way.

"Talking of witches," said Mr Brown,
looking very serious, "do you know how
a witch tells the time?"

"With a witch-watch," said Hamlet,
who always enjoyed a good joke. (He
enjoyed a bad joke too, which was lucky
because most of Mr Brown's jokes were
very bad indeed. The next he tried was
one of his worst.)

"Why do witches ride broomsticks?"

Hamlet didn't know the answer to this one. "I don't know. Why do witches ride broomsticks?"

"Because vacuum cleaners don't have long-enough flexes!" said Mr Brown, and he burst out laughing.

Hamlet laughed too, although he wasn't sure that he understood the joke.

Mr Brown thought his next joke was the funniest of all. "Did you hear about the witch who had been ill? The doctor came to see her. He felt her pulse. He took her temperature. He said, 'I am glad to say you're much better. You can get up for a spell this afternoon.'"

"I don't get it," said Hamlet.

"You're so stupid," said Susan. "Witches cast spells. That's how they make their magic work."

Hamlet couldn't think of anything

rude enough to say to his sister, so he
stuck his tongue out at her instead.

When they arrived at the library, Mr
Brown was still chuckling. He marched
straight up to the counter.

"Good morning, librarian," he said.

"Good morning," said the librarian,
looking at Mr Brown a little suspiciously.
"Can I help you?"

"I hope so," said Mr Brown. "Do you
by any chance have a book called *Droopy
Drawers*?"

"*Droopy Drawers*," repeated the
librarian, frowning. "That's a funny title."

"It's a funny book," said Mr Brown.

"Who is it by?" asked the librarian.

"Lucy Lastick," said Mr Brown.

"*Droopy Drawers* by Lucy Lastick," repeated the librarian.

"Oh, Dad," groaned Susan.

"Just my little joke," said Mr Brown. "It's a silly title I made up. Like *Down in the Forest* by Theresa Green."

"I don't think we've got that one either," said the librarian, who was not amused. "Is there anything else I can do for you?"

"Yes, please," said Susan. "I am looking for books on witches and witchcraft."

"And I want a book on how to train your beagle," said Hamlet.

"Come with me," said the librarian, and she led the children off towards the bookshelves.

"I'll wait here," said Mr Brown, "and read the notices."

The first notice that caught Mr Brown's eyes was the largest. It said:

CALLING ALL ARTISTS

On Saturday 31 October at Hammersmith Library there will be a special exhibition of paintings and drawings by local artists. If you would like to enter a painting for the exhibition, please bring it to the library no later than 10.00 a.m. on 31 October. The celebrated art critic Mrs Verna Hanley will act as judge, and certificates and book tokens will be awarded for the best pictures.

I might enter that, thought Mr Brown.

"Have you ever had your portrait painted, Puddles?"

Puddles gave a little bark.

"You haven't? I didn't think so. Well, now's your chance. I'll get out my old oil-paints this week and have a go."

Puddles gave a louder bark.

"Who knows, we might even win!"

Puddles began wagging his tail and yapping happily.

"Ssh," said the librarian who had come back with Hamlet and Susan and a pile of books. "Please don't make so much noise."

"So sorry," said Mr Brown.

"Woof," said Puddles. "Woof-woof."

"Can't you see the sign?" said the librarian, looking very frosty and pointing to the large notice marked SILENCE.

"Of course I can see it," said Mr Brown. "The problem is Puddles. Believe it or not, he can't read!"

Clearly Puddles thought this was a very good joke because he started yapping even more loudly and began jumping up and down like a big bouncing ball.

"Come on, Dad," said Susan. "I think we'd better go."

"Thank you for your help," Mr Brown said to the librarian. "I'll be back for the painting competition next Saturday."

"Oh good," said the librarian. But she didn't mean it.

"Be sure to keep a space for my

picture," said Mr Brown rather grandly. "It is going to be a portrait of Puddles."

"It's Hallowe'en next Saturday," said Susan as they walked down the library steps.

"What fun!" said Mr Brown.

"What's so special about Hallowe'en?" asked Hamlet.

"That's when the witches come to call," said Susan in a mysterious voice.

"I don't believe in witches," said Hamlet very firmly.

3. Puddles Makes a Splash

After lunch, Susan settled down at the kitchen table with her books and Hamlet took Puddles out into the back garden for his first lesson. The librarian had found Hamlet exactly what he needed. It was a small book called *Easy Ways to Train Your Beagle* and on the cover was a photograph of a beagle puppy that looked very like Puddles.

"Now, you've got to pay attention, Puddles," said Hamlet seriously. "If we don't get you trained by this time next week you're in trouble."

Puddles wagged his tail.

"Listen to this." Hamlet had opened the book and was reading the first sentence. "The merry beagle is a most attractive and conveniently sized hound." Puddles began to jump up and down.

"He is lively and bouncy and full of energy."

Puddles was certainly all of that.

"He needs regular exercise and proper training, or he will get up to mischief."

Puddles felt like getting up to some mischief right away, so he ran to the little flowerbed at the bottom of the garden and began to dig up one of Mr Brown's favourite plants.

"Naughty, Puddles," shouted Hamlet. "Stop it, stop it!"

Puddles must have understood that Hamlet wasn't pleased because he stopped digging.

"Come here at once," said Hamlet. Puddles trotted over, wagging his tail. "It says here, 'A puppy can be taught to recognize the word 'sit' and obey it from

as early as twelve weeks.' You're older
than twelve weeks, Puddles, aren't
you?"

Puddles barked happily. Hamlet went
on reading. "To get your puppy to sit,
press your hands down gently on his
hips and at the same time tell him to 'sit'.
Keep pressing down until your puppy
understands what you want."

Puddles thought he understood what
Hamlet wanted. Puddles thought Hamlet
wanted to play. Hamlet pressed down
gently on Puddles's hips and Puddles
put his front paws up on Hamlet's
shoulders.

"Sit," said Hamlet fiercely.

"Woof," barked Puddles happily.

"Sit," said Hamlet, pressing down even more firmly.

"Woof-woof," went Puddles even more happily, and he jumped up against Hamlet and began to lick his face.

"Stop it, Puddles," said Hamlet. "It tickles! Stop it!" But Puddles didn't stop it. He was having too much fun.

"You're tickling me, Puddles. Stop it," called Hamlet, and as he made one last attempt to get his puppy to sit, Hamlet slipped and landed flat on his back.

"Sit!" he shouted for the very last time and lo and behold, wonder of wonders, all of a sudden Puddles did sit!

"Good boy!" cried Hamlet, flat on his back, but as pleased as pleased could be. He was about to sit up and give Puddles a pat on the head, when he noticed a light go on in one of the upstairs windows at the back of the house. There was nothing unusual about that. What was unusual was what the light revealed. It was a witch. It really was.

Lying flat on his back on the patch of grass in the little garden of No. 13 Irving Terrace, Hammersmith, West London, Hamlet Brown could not believe his eyes. He closed them. He opened them. There was no mistake. Up on the first floor,

standing right by the window, was a witch. She had a pointed witch's hat on her head and a broomstick in her hand. What on earth was she doing there?

Hamlet forgot all about Puddles. He scrambled to his feet and ran into the house.

"Susan! Susan!" he called.

"Yes, what is it?" Susan called back from the kitchen.

"I've seen a – " He hesitated. After all, it was only a matter of hours since he'd told his sister he didn't believe in witches.

Susan looked up from the book she was reading.

"What is it?" she said impatiently. "Can't you see I'm busy?"

"Sorry," said Hamlet, and he ran out of the kitchen and up the stairs.

There were four rooms on the first

floor at No. 13 Irving Terrace. Hamlet's room and Mr and Mrs Brown's room were at the front of the house. Susan's room and the spare room were at the back. Hamlet could hear Mrs Brown reading out loud in the spare room. The witch must be in Susan's room. Susan had put a notice on her door. It said:

THIS ROOM BELONGS TO
SUSAN BROWN
DO NOT ENTER –
ESPECIALLY IF YOU ARE
CALLED HAMLET

Slowly, carefully, quietly, Hamlet turned the door handle. As the door creaked open, Hamlet peered inside. The room was dark. Hamlet thought he saw a shadowy figure standing by the window, but he wasn't sure. Hamlet found the light switch. He flicked it. The light came on. There was no one there.

Suddenly he felt a heavy hand on his shoulder.

"Gotcha!" said Mr Brown.

Hamlet jumped. "Goodness, Dad, you gave me a fright."

"I'm sorry, my boy, but I wondered what you were up to in Susan's room."

"Nothing," said Hamlet quickly.

"Really?" Mr Brown raised his right eyebrow.

"Yes, really." Hamlet hesitated. "Well, no, I was looking for something."

"And what was that?" asked Mr Brown.

"Er . . . nothing," said Hamlet.

"You were doing nothing, looking for nothing," said Mr Brown. "That sounds interesting."

"Actually," said Hamlet, who had now

given himself enough time to think of a
good excuse, "I was looking for
Puddles."

"He's not likely to be up here, is he?"
said Mr Brown, who didn't find Hamlet's
story very convincing.

"Er, actually," said Hamlet, "I think
he's in the garden."

"What's he doing there?" asked Mr
Brown, who was really quite confused.

"I've been teaching him to sit," said
Hamlet.

"And how have you been getting on?"
asked Mr Brown.

"I've done it," said Hamlet proudly.

"Really?" said Mr Brown, raising both eyebrows now.

"Really!" said Hamlet. "Follow me!" And Hamlet scampered down the stairs and out into the garden. Mr Brown followed.

Puddles was digging up another of Mr Brown's favourite plants.

"Puddles!" called Hamlet. Puddles looked up.

"Puddles," said Hamlet sternly, "sit!"

And the moment Hamlet said "sit", Puddles sat.

"Bravo!" cried Mr Brown. "This is most impressive. I think it's time for his next lesson."

"What's that?"

"Retrieving," said Mr Brown, with considerable authority.

"What's retrieving?" asked Hamlet.

"We'll take Puddles to the park," said Mr Brown, "and I'll show you."

When they got to the park Puddles was so excited that the moment Mr Brown let him off the lead, he began running round and round in circles chasing his own tail.

"Sit!" commanded Hamlet fiercely. Puddles didn't hear him. "Sit!" Hamlet shouted more loudly. Puddles sat.

"Good dog!" said Hamlet.

"He's a fast learner," said Mr Brown, picking up a stick from the ground. "Now we'll put him to the test. I'm going to throw this stick for him and we want him to bring it back to us. It's called retrieving."

Mr Brown threw the stick a little distance in front of them. Puddles picked up the idea right away. He ran to the stick, lifted it with his mouth and brought it straight back to Hamlet and Mr Brown.

"You throw this time," Mr Brown said to his son.

Hamlet threw it a little bit further. Puddles ran to collect it and brought it straight back.

"Good dog!" said Hamlet.

"My turn now," said Mr Brown. This time he flung the stick high and hard and Hamlet and Puddles watched it sail through the air and land, splash, right in the middle of the pond.

"No, Puddles, no!" called out Mr Brown.

"Sit, Puddles, sit!" shouted Hamlet, but it was too late. Puddles was on his way, running as fast as his four little legs would carry him.

"He can't swim! He can't swim!" shouted Hamlet, as the beagle puppy flung himself headfirst into the pond.

"He can swim!" gasped Mr Brown in amazement, as Puddles paddled his way towards the stick.

Puddles reached the piece of wood

bobbing in the water, grabbed hold of it with his jaw, spun round and paddled back to the edge of the pond.

"Good dog!" cheered Hamlet, as he helped Mr Brown haul Puddles out of the water.

"Naughty dog!" said Mrs Brown, as Mr Brown and Hamlet and a dripping wet Puddles came into the kitchen at No. 13 Irving Terrace twenty minutes later.

"What has he been up to?" asked Susan, who was still sitting at the kitchen table working on her project.

"He's been swimming in the pond," said Hamlet.

"It's all part of his training," explained Mr Brown. "He's well on his way to becoming a fully-trained animal. He's very clever."

"He's very wet!" said Mrs Brown.

To prove the point, Puddles decided to

42

give himself a good shake.

Susan let out a shriek. "He's splashing water all over my books! Get him to stop!"

"Sit, Puddles!" ordered Hamlet. "Sit!"

Unfortunately Puddles didn't seem to hear Hamlet's command. He went on giving himself a good shake, spraying the dirty pond water everywhere.

"He's ruining my project!" yelped Susan.

"Stop it, Puddles!" said Mr Brown.

"If he doesn't stop I'll use one of my spells on him," said Susan.

"Sit!" said Mrs Brown very loudly and very fiercely. "Sit!"

When Mrs Brown gave the order, Puddles did as he was told.

4. The Broomstick at No. 13

On Sunday morning Hamlet Orlando Julius Caesar Brown woke up late and went down to breakfast half asleep.

He was halfway down the stairs when he stopped. He had just passed something on the landing that shouldn't have been there. Had he imagined it? Was he dreaming? Slowly he turned round and there, propped up in the corner of the landing, as large as life, was a witch's broomstick.

Hamlet ran down the stairs and into the kitchen. Susan was sitting at the table working on her project.

"Where's Mum?" asked Hamlet.

"I think she's doing her recording for Mrs Mayhew."

"Where's Dad?"

"I don't know."

"Where's Puddles?"

"I don't know and I don't care. He made a terrible mess of my drawing of the witch's cauldron yesterday. I've had to start all over again."

"Can I have a look?" asked Hamlet.

"If you want to," said Susan, rather surprised. Her brother didn't usually take any interest in her work.

"It's a witch's lair!" Susan explained. "That's the cauldron. That's the witch's book of spells. That's her besom."

"It looks like a broomstick to me," said

Hamlet, thinking it looked *exactly* like the broomstick now standing on the landing at No. 13 Irving Terrace, Hammersmith, West London.

"It is a broomstick," said Susan.

"Why did you call it whatever you called it then?" asked Hamlet.

"Because that's its proper name."

"Have you ever seen a real witch's broomstick?" asked Hamlet.

"Only in pictures," said Susan.

"I've seen a real one," said Hamlet.

"Don't be stupid," said his sister.

"I have," Hamlet persisted.

"Where?"

"I'll show you." And Hamlet grabbed his sister by the wrist and led her out into the hallway.

"Look."

Sure enough, at the top of the stairs, leaning against the wall on the landing was a besom that looked exactly like the one in Susan's picture.

"Where did that come from?" asked Susan.

"I don't know," said Hamlet.

The pair of them climbed the stairs to take a closer look.

"Do you think it works?" said Hamlet.

"What do you mean?"

"Do you think it flies?"

"Don't be stupid," said Susan. "It isn't really a witch's broomstick."

"How do you know?" asked Hamlet.

"Witches aren't real, stupid."

"How do you know?" repeated
Hamlet.

"Everyone knows that," said Susan.

Hamlet picked up the broomstick. It
was much heavier than he'd expected.
He put one leg over it.

"What are you doing?" asked Susan.

"I'm going to see if it flies."

"Don't, Hamlet. It's dangerous."

"Here goes," said Hamlet, standing

with his feet on either side of the broomstick at the top of the stairs. "One, two, three and – "

"Stop!" shouted Susan.

"What on earth are you two doing?" asked Mrs Brown, who had come out of the spare room.

"Nothing," said Hamlet.

"Well, don't make so much noise while you're about it," said Mrs Brown. "And kindly leave my besom alone. It's not a toy, you know."

"Sorry, Mum," said Hamlet, climbing off the broomstick and handing it over to his mother. "I thought it was a wit – "

"Never mind what you thought," interrupted Mrs Brown. "You were making a good deal too much noise. Have you had your breakfast yet?"

"No, Mum," said Hamlet.

"Well, hurry along and get it and let

me get on with my recording," said Mrs Brown.

"Yes, Mum."

Mrs Brown went back into the spare room and Hamlet and Susan went back downstairs to the kitchen.

"Don't you believe in witches then?" Hamlet asked his sister as he poured himself a bowl of cornflakes.

"Of course not."

"But I thought they used to burn witches?"

"They burnt people they *thought* were witches," explained Susan.

"What about the spells then? Didn't they work?"

"Some people believed they worked, but they didn't really. Witches are like ghosts. They don't exist."

Hamlet didn't say anything. Hamlet was sure he had seen a real ghost once and he was sure that yesterday he had seen a real witch. If Susan didn't believe in ghosts and witches, that was up to her. Hamlet knew what he had seen with his own eyes.

Now he knew what he could hear with his own ears. It was Puddles barking, and it wasn't a gentle, friendly, good-morning-how-are-you-I'm-Puddles sort of bark. It was an urgent, angry, fierce bark and it was coming from the hallway.

"Puddles has seen the witch," shouted Hamlet.

"Don't be ridiculous," said Susan.

But Hamlet wasn't listening. He had already run out of the kitchen and into the hallway. He looked up the stairs and there, on the landing, was a ladder leading to the loft. On almost the top step of the ladder, Hamlet could see a strange pair of feet. At the foot of the ladder was Puddles, barking furiously.

"Attack!" shouted Hamlet. "Attack!" Puddles obeyed the order.

"Help!" shouted a familiar voice from the attic and with a terrible bang, crash, wallop, woof, Mr Brown and Puddles came tumbling down the ladder and landed in a heap on the landing.

"What is it this time?" said Mrs

Brown, coming out of the spare room.
She looked very cross indeed.

"Sorry, Mum," said Hamlet.

"Sorry, my sweet," said Mr Brown,
stumbling to his feet.

"Woof," said Puddles, wagging his tail
happily.

"I was just looking for my old artist's
easel in the attic," explained Mr Brown,
"and Puddles must have thought I was
an intruder. He's going to be a very
useful watchdog. We should be grateful
really."

"I'd be grateful if I could be left in
peace to finish recording the book for
Mrs Mayhew," said Mrs Brown with a
sigh. "It's not a lot to ask, is it?"

"No, my sweet," said Mr Brown, who
always liked to keep Mrs Brown happy.
"We'll go downstairs now and be as
quiet as mice."

Mr Brown and Hamlet and Puddles crept down to the kitchen.

"Did you catch your witch?" asked Susan.

Hamlet stuck his tongue out at his sister and put a piece of bread in the toaster. Mr Brown began to set up his easel.

"If I am going to paint a portrait of you, Puddles, you're going to have to sit very, very still for me," said Mr Brown. "Do you understand?"

"Woof," said Puddles.

"He should really be saying 'Tick-woof-tock-woof', shouldn't he?" said Mr Brown.

"Tick-woof-tock-woof?" asked Susan. "What kind of dog goes 'Tick-woof-tock-woof'?"

"A watch-dog, of course," said Mr Brown with a chuckle.

5. The Vanishing Witch

On Monday afternoon, when Susan and Hamlet came home from school, they found Mr Brown in a very good mood. He had started his painting of Puddles and he had thought of a new joke.

"Susan," he said, dipping one of his brushes into a little pot of bright green paint, "what is green and goes boing-boing?"

"A green boing-boing?" suggested Susan.

"Quite right," said Mr Brown with a laugh. He rinsed the brush in a jar of water and dipped it into the little pot of red paint.

"Hamlet, what's red and goes boing-boing?"

"A red boing-boing?" said Hamlet, hoping he had got the right idea.

"Excellent," said Mr Brown, cleaning his brush again. "Susan, what's yellow and goes boing-boing?"

"A yellow boing-boing," said Susan confidently.

"Oh no," said Mr Brown. "They don't make them in that colour! I thought everybody knew that!"

Susan groaned. Hamlet laughed.

"I apologize," said Mr Brown. "I know it's a very bad joke, but I just couldn't help it. I think it must be the snoo I put in my coffee at lunchtime."

"What's snoo?" asked Hamlet.

"Nothing much," said Mr Brown. "What's new with you?"

"Oh, Dad," said Susan. "Your jokes are terrible."

"I know," said Mr Brown. "But my

painting's brilliant, don't you think?"

Hamlet and Susan did not know what to say. On Mr Brown's artist's easel was a very large piece of paper with, in the middle of it, a very large splodge of brown paint.

"Come on," said Mr Brown. "Tell me the truth. What do you think of it so far?"

Hamlet hesitated. "It's very good but, er – "

"It doesn't look much like Puddles," said Susan bravely.

"Quite right, my girl. It's early days. I'm just working on the background. You have got to get the background right first. By this time tomorrow it will look quite different."

It did. When Hamlet and Susan got home from school on Tuesday, they found that the splodge had got larger and had changed from brown to green.

"I started all over again," explained Mr Brown. "I decided to paint Puddles in the garden. That's the grass."

"Where's Puddles?" asked Hamlet.

"Upstairs, I think," said Mr Brown.

"No," said Hamlet. "I meant where is he in the picture?"

"Oh, he isn't in the picture yet," said Mr Brown. "I've got to get the background right first."

By Wednesday afternoon Mr Brown had changed the background again. It was blue this time.

"I have decided to do a picture of

Puddles swimming in the pond. I think it will make it more unusual, don't you?"

"Yes," said Susan.

"Definitely," said Hamlet.

"It will also mean that I only have to paint his head," explained Mr Brown. "If he's supposed to be swimming you wouldn't expect to see his body. It's rather a clever idea of mine, don't you think?"

"Very clever," said Susan.

"Shall I get him?" asked Hamlet.

"Yes, please," said Mr Brown. "I think he's in the garden."

Hamlet went to fetch Puddles. As he was crossing the hallway he heard a noise coming from upstairs. It was a dog, barking. Hamlet ran up the stairs.

The barking seemed to be coming from the spare room. Hamlet had his hand on the door-handle and was about to turn it and go in, when he heard something else. It was the sound of an old woman cackling.

The witch is in there, thought Hamlet, and she's got Puddles. She's probably turning him into a frog right now. I've got to rescue him.

"It's all right, Puddles," Hamlet said bravely. "I'm here." And he turned the handle and burst into the spare room. He expected to find the witch with her broomstick under one arm and Puddles under the other. Instead, he found his mother reading out loud the book she was recording for old Mrs Mayhew at No. 17.

"Where's Puddles?" said Hamlet.

"I don't know," said Mrs Brown. "I thought your father was painting him in the kitchen."

"Isn't he in here?" asked Hamlet.

"No," said Mrs Brown. "See for yourself."

Hamlet looked under the spare bed and behind the armchair. He even opened the big cupboard in the corner. Puddles definitely wasn't there.

"That's very odd," he said. "I'm sure I heard Puddles in here. And not just Puddles."

"You must have been imagining things," said Mrs Brown with a smile.

Hamlet shook his head. Something very strange was going on. What could it all mean?

Just then, Susan shouted up the stairs, "We've found him!"

Hamlet ran down to Susan who was holding Puddles at the bottom of the stairs.

"Where was he?"

"In the garden, of course."

"Are you sure?"

"Of course I'm sure. He was trying to dig up the lavender bush, the naughty little puppy."

"Susan," said Hamlet very seriously. "Do you know everything about witches?"

"I don't know everything," said Susan modestly. "Not yet, anyway."

"Do you know if they can make themselves disappear?"

"I don't know about that," said Susan.

"I do," said Mr Brown, appearing suddenly at the kitchen doorway and making both his children jump. (Puddles jumped too, but only because Susan was holding him.)

"Some years ago your dear mother and I appeared together in a wonderful play about a Scottish king called Macbeth. It is a very spooky play and in it three witches come to visit Macbeth."

"On broomsticks?" said Hamlet.

"No," said Mr Brown. "Not on broomsticks. That's the point. These witches just appeared and disappeared. One moment you saw them, the next you didn't. They vanished into thin air."

"The wicked witch in *The Wizard of Oz* had a broomstick," said Susan.

"Oh yes," said Mr Brown. "Most witches do travel by broomstick, but not all of them."

"And most witches have a black cat too," said Susan.

"Absolutely correct," said Mr Brown.

"Have you ever heard of a witch having a beagle puppy?" asked Hamlet anxiously.

"No, I haven't," said Mr Brown. "What a funny idea. Would you like to be a witch's dog, Puddles?"

Puddles went "Woof" and disappeared. He didn't vanish in a puff of smoke. He jumped smartly out of Susan's arms and scampered off into the garden.

6. "I've Seen a Witch!"

When Susan and Hamlet got home from school on Thursday afternoon, they found Mrs Brown in the kitchen. She was making gingerbread.

"Are you going to make gingerbread men?" asked Hamlet, who loved gingerbread.

"No," said Mrs Brown. "I'm making gingerbread cats. Look."

Hamlet looked at the row of cats that Mrs Brown had cut out of gingerbread and placed on her baking tray. They looked exactly like witches' cats.

"While your father's painting a dog, I thought I'd bake a cat!" said Mrs Brown with a smile.

"Where *is* Dad?" asked Susan.

"Where's Puddles?" asked Hamlet.

"They're both upstairs," said Mrs Brown, her smile turning into a frown, "in the bathroom."

Hamlet and Susan ran out of the kitchen and up the stairs. The bathroom door was shut. From inside came the sound of Puddles growling and Mr Brown singing. Hamlet thought to himself, When we open the door will they still be there?

Susan knocked on the bathroom door. "Can we come in?"

"If you can get in, yes," called Mr Brown. "It's a bit of a squeeze in here."

Susan opened the door and she and Hamlet peered inside. Mr Brown was there all right and so was Puddles. Mr Brown was wearing his artist's smock and his artist's floppy hat and was holding his paintbrush between his teeth. He was on his hands and knees.

"What are you doing, Dad?" asked
Hamlet.

"Just mopping up," said Mr Brown
casually, as he pushed a large towel
across the sopping wet bathroom floor.
"I'm afraid Puddles isn't helping."

Puddles, in fact, was too busy to help.
He was rolling round in one of Mrs
Brown's very best bathroom towels.

"Is this one of Puddles' puddles?"
asked Susan, wide-eyed as she looked at
the soaking floor.

"Oh no," said Mr Brown. "*I* did it!
Well, Puddles and I did it between us."

"What do you mean, Dad?" asked Susan.

"Well," explained Mr Brown. "Since I was going to paint a picture of Puddles swimming in the pond, I thought it would be a good idea to get him to pose for me in the bath."

"Do you mean – " Hamlet stammered.

"Yes," said Mr Brown happily. "I filled up the bath and then popped Puddles in, but he didn't seem to like the idea. Perhaps the water was too hot. Anyway, no sooner had I put him in than he managed to jump out and bring rather a lot of bath-water with him."

"Oh, Dad," said Susan.

"Oh, Puddles," said Hamlet.

"Oh dear," said Mrs Brown, who had joined them at the bathroom door.

"Oh well," said Mr Brown with a sigh. "I'll just have to start all over again."

And he did. By the time Hamlet and Susan got back from school on Friday, Mr Brown had painted a new background – bright yellow this time – and had even begun to sketch in the outline of the beagle puppy.

"Even if I have to work all through the night," he announced over tea, "I shall finish this portrait of Puddles by the time the library opens tomorrow morning."

After tea, Susan went to her room to get on with her project and Hamlet stayed in the kitchen to help his father.

"All I want you to do, my boy, is persuade that naughty little puppy of yours to sit still."

"Sit!" Hamlet ordered. Puddles sat.

"Excellent!" cried Mr Brown. "Now, don't move."

For a moment Puddles didn't move, but it wasn't a very long moment. It was just long enough for Mr Brown to dip his paintbrush into the little pot of brown paint. By the time Mr Brown was ready to apply his paintbrush to the paper, Puddles was chasing his tail again.

"Sit!" shouted Hamlet. Puddles sat, and this time he stayed sitting for what seemed like quite a long time. Unfortunately, although he was definitely sitting, he wasn't sitting very still.

"How can I paint him if he keeps fidgeting and scratching himself like that!" exclaimed an exasperated Mr Brown. "What am I going to do?"

"*I* know," said Hamlet all of a sudden. "I'll get the book – *Easy Ways to Train Your Beagle*. It's got a big photograph of a puppy just like Puddles on the cover. You can copy that."

"Child," said Mr Brown, taking off his floppy artist's hat and bowing to his son, "you are a genius. My problem is solved. Puddles, you may chase your tail and scratch yourself as much as you please. Hamlet, kindly fetch the book at once."

Hamlet ran out of the kitchen and up the stairs to his room. The book was on the floor by the foot of his bed. He picked it up, turned, cheerfully swung out of his room, and then, as he reached the top of the stairway, he saw her. She really was there, with her black cloak and her pointed black hat and a broomstick in her hand. The witch he had seen at the window was now standing in the little hallway at the foot of the stairs with her back to him. Hamlet stepped back so that if she turned she wouldn't see him.

When she did turn, Hamlet could see her quite clearly. Her face was all green and knobbly, like an ugly mask. He held his breath as, slowly, the witch began to climb the stairs. He pulled himself right back into the corner so she wouldn't catch sight of him. When she got to the top of the stairs she walked straight towards the spare room. As she opened the door she took off her pointed hat and Hamlet saw Mrs Brown inside the room, smiling at her.

The moment the witch had closed the spare-room door behind her, Hamlet ran

down the stairs as fast as his legs would
carry him. He burst into the kitchen.

"My goodness, Hamlet," said Mr
Brown. "You look as if you've seen a
ghost."

"I've seen a witch!" gasped Hamlet,
"and she's upstairs with Mum."

"Don't be ridiculous," said Mr Brown.

"It's true," said Hamlet. "I'll show
you. Come on!"

And Hamlet and his father, with

Puddles in tow, made their way upstairs. Hamlet knocked boldly on the spare-room door. There was no answer.

"In we go," said Mr Brown.

"Be careful!" said Hamlet.

"Woof!" said Puddles.

Slowly Mr Brown turned the door handle and pushed open the spare-room door. The room was empty. There was no sign of any witch. There was no sign of Mrs Brown, either. Hamlet looked under the bed again. He looked behind the armchair. He looked inside the cupboard. He even looked behind the big mirror on the wall facing the door. There was no one there.

"Where's your witch, my boy?" asked Mr Brown, raising an eyebrow as he looked at his son.

"Where's Mum?" asked Hamlet, who was suddenly frightened. Had the witch

74

put his mother on the back of her
broomstick and flown off with her to
some horrible witch's lair? "Where is
she?"

"I'm here," said Mrs Brown, coming
out of her bedroom and crossing the
landing. "Where did you think I was?"

7. The Witch at No. 13

Saturday turned out to be rather a special day for everyone at No. 13 Irving Terrace, Hammersmith, West London. It began with a treat. Mr Brown decided to give the family breakfast in bed.

When Mr Brown made breakfast in bed, Hamlet and Susan were allowed to sit on the end of their parents' bed to have it. Normally, Mr Brown was very cheerful in the morning (normally, Mr Brown was very cheerful all the time), but the moment their father came into the bedroom carrying the breakfast tray, Hamlet and Susan could see he was unhappy.

"What's wrong, Dad?" asked Susan.

"Everything," said Mr Brown. "I've spilt the coffee."

"Never mind," said Mrs Brown
soothingly.

"I've burnt the toast."

"I like burnt toast," said Hamlet
helpfully.

"We've run out of honey."

"I like jam better," said Susan.

"And the dog's ruined my painting."

"Oh dear," said Mrs Brown. "So that's
the matter. What's he done?"

"He's walked all over it," said Mr
Brown. "I didn't finish it till nearly
midnight. I left it lying out on the kitchen

77

table so that the paint would dry, and that naughty puppy must have climbed up on to the table and walked all over it. The picture's ruined."

"I'm sure it's not that bad," said Mrs Brown who, secretly, hadn't thought it was very good to begin with. "Let's have a look at it."

Mr Brown went and fetched his painting. It was covered with muddy paw-prints.

"I think it looks good," said Hamlet.

"I think it looks terrible," said Mr Brown.

Mrs Brown didn't say anything.

"I can't enter it for the art competition now," said Mr Brown sadly, crunching on a bit of dry, burnt toast.

"Yes you can," said Hamlet.

"You must, Dad," said Susan. "You told the librarian that you'd definitely be bringing in a picture. I think you've got to."

"And I want you all out of the house anyway," said Mrs Brown.

"What's going on, Mum?" asked Hamlet.

"Never you mind," said Mrs Brown.

"It's something to do with that witch, isn't it?" said Hamlet.

"There isn't any witch," said Susan. "I wish there were."

"That reminds me," said Mr Brown. "Today's Hallowe'en, isn't it?"

"Today," said Mrs Brown, "is a day when I need the house to myself."

"What for, Mum?" asked Hamlet, who was absolutely certain he hadn't been imagining things when he saw his mother meet the witch.

"That's my little secret," said Mrs Brown with a mysterious smile. "You

can come back at four o'clock, but not a
minute before. That's an order."

And when Mrs Brown gave an order,
everyone at No. 13 obeyed. As soon as
they were dressed and the breakfast
things had been cleared away, Mr Brown
and Susan and Hamlet set off.

First they went to the library and
handed in Mr Brown's painting. The
librarian took it and held it up. She
looked at it with a rather surprised
expression. "It's . . . er, er . . . very

interesting," she said with a little cough. "What is it?"

"It's upside down at the moment," said Mr Brown. "When it's the right way up it's supposed to be a dog."

"Oh, I'm so sorry," said the librarian, turning the picture round the other way. "Oh yes, of course, now I can see. That must be his nose?"

"No," said Mr Brown. "That's his tail."

"Oh dear," said the librarian. "I was never very good with modern art. Anyway, thank you for bringing it. I've kept a space for it on the wall over here. Be sure to be back by three."

"What's happening then?" asked Susan.

"That's when Mrs Hanley is doing the judging and giving out the prizes."

"I don't think I'll be winning any

prizes," sighed Mr Brown.

"Well, perhaps not," said the librarian, looking at the picture again, "but you can see who does. We've had some wonderful paintings entered for the exhibition."

The librarian was right. Some of the paintings were very good indeed. Susan particularly liked a beautiful snow scene. Hamlet liked the life-sized portrait of a clown. Mr Brown could tell that they were all much better than his.

After they had looked at the other pictures, they set off for the shops. Mrs Brown had given them a very long shopping list. She had also given them permission to have lunch at McDonald's. Because Puddles wasn't allowed into the restaurant, they had takeaway meals and ate them on a bench in the park.

Just before three o'clock they made

their way back to the library.

"I don't know why we're bothering to go," said Mr Brown rather sadly.

"It would be rude not to," said Susan.

"Woof," barked Puddles.

"I'm not speaking to you," said Mr Brown. "You ruined my picture."

When they arrived they found quite a crowd at the library and Mrs Hanley was already in the middle of the judging.

"And now," she said, "we come to the animal paintings. There have been some lovely entries in this category this year. I particularly admired the African lion painted by Mrs Bowis of Barnes, and Sophie Curry of Putney submitted a very charming study of three newly born kittens. But I have to tell you, ladies and gentlemen, that the moment I came into the library my eye was caught by one picture and by one picture alone. It is a picture of a dog."

Mr Brown gasped. Susan and Hamlet held their breath. Puddles began to wag his tail.

"Between you and me," continued Mrs Hanley, "I have seen better pictures of dogs, but I have never before come across an artist who had the bright idea of covering his painting with paw-prints. That is why, for sheer originality, the first prize has to go to Mr Brown of Hammersmith."

Everyone began to clap. Hamlet and Susan cheered. Mr Brown picked up

Puddles and gave him an enormous hug.

"That's my beagle," he said as, proudly, man and dog stepped forward to collect the special certificate and book-token prize from Mrs Hanley.

The little group that made its way back to No. 13 Irving Terrace that afternoon was in a better mood than it had been when it set out that morning.

"I am so happy," said Mr Brown, "I feel like having a party, don't you?"

"Oh yes," chorused Hamlet and Susan.

Just then they turned into Irving

Terrace. It was dark now, but they could see their house clearly because in one of the upstairs windows there was a face shining at them brightly. It wasn't a human face. It was a face cut out of a pumpkin.

When they reached the front door they could hear strange noises coming from inside. There were giggles and cackles and screams. Hamlet thought he heard barking. Puddles did too. He pricked up his ears.

"What's going on here?" Mr Brown wondered out loud.

He had just put his key into the lock, when the front door opened and there she was: the witch. Hamlet recognized her at once. He had seen that pointed hat and that cloak and that broomstick and that knobbly green face before.

"Happy Hallowe'en!" said the witch.

"Who are you?" said Mr Brown, stepping back at the frightening sight.

"I am the witch at No. 13," cackled the witch.

Puddles looked up at her and began to growl.

"I don't think we should go in," said Susan, as a terrifying screaming noise came down the stairs.

"Nor do I," said Hamlet nervously.

"Don't worry," chuckled the witch, taking off her pointed hat. "It's only me." Attached to the hat was the witch's

mask and underneath it was a face they all recognized: Mrs Brown's.

"Oh, Mum!" sighed Susan. "You gave us quite a fright."

"What a performance!" exclaimed Mr Brown, who was very proud of his wife's skill as an actress.

"I can't believe it," said Hamlet. "Was it you all along?"

"Yes," said Mrs Brown. "It was Susan's project that gave me the idea. I thought it would be fun to dress up as a witch and plan a surprise party for us all for Hallowe'en."

"So you were the witch standing at the window?" asked Hamlet.

"Yes," said Mrs Brown. "That was when I tried on the costume for the first time."

"And you made all the spooky noises?"

"Yes," said Mrs Brown. "I made a tape of them while you were out at school. Puddles helped me. That's why he's on the tape too."

"Woof," said Puddles, recognizing his own name.

"I'm glad I managed to make it a real surprise," said Mrs Brown. "I was sure Hamlet was going to find me out."

"There's something I still don't understand," said Hamlet. "Yesterday, when I watched the witch coming up the stairs, I saw her open the door to the spare room and you were already inside."

"Oh no I wasn't," said Mrs Brown.

"But I saw you standing inside the room, Mum," said Hamlet.

"You *think* you saw me standing inside the room," said Mrs Brown, "but I was outside, and as I opened the door to go in I took off the witch's hat and mask and what you saw was the reflection of my face in the mirror!"

Hamlet did not know what to say. Puddles could not think what to say either.

"I may not be a real witch," said Mrs Brown, "but I think you'll like my witch's tea. Follow me."

She led the way to the kitchen, where Hamlet and Susan and Mr Brown and Puddles feasted their eyes on a table covered with good things. Right in the middle was a cake shaped like a witch's cauldron and around it were plates and bowls piled high with little cakes and biscuits, chocolates and crisps, sandwiches, and sausages on sticks. There were green jellies and yellow jellies and a delicious blue-coloured drink that Mrs Brown said was a special witch's brew. Best of all, there were gingerbread cats, dozens of them. Hamlet ate eleven of them and Puddles had three.

"Puddles is being very well-behaved," said Mrs Brown, when she saw the beagle puppy sitting up and begging for another gingerbread cat.

Puddles wagged his tail.

"It's over a week since he made a puddle," said Hamlet.

"And he helped Dad win the art competition," said Susan.

"Really?" said Mrs Brown. "Well, I think we'd better let him stay, don't you?"

"Woof," said Puddles.

"That's the best news I've ever heard!" said Hamlet.

"And this is the best Hallowe'en party we've ever had," said Mr Brown.

"It's the *only* one we've ever had," said Susan.

"I won't forget it," said Hamlet.

"I hope not," said Mrs Brown.

"I'll make sure no one forgets it," said Mr Brown. "Tomorrow I'm going to paint another picture."

"What are you going to paint this time?" asked Hamlet.

"Can't you guess?" said Mr Brown with a chuckle. "I'm going to paint the witch at No. 13!"